To Paula, Zizo, and Vani.

— R. M.

THE VERY HUNGRY PLANT

RENATO MORICONI

EERDMANS BOOKS FOR YOUNG READERS

GRAND RAPIDS, MICHIGAN

One beautiful morning, a little plant sprouted.

And it was
hungry!

But the sun
didn't satisfy
its hunger...

...because
it was a
carnivorous
plant.

That's why
it ate a
caterpillar
that was
passing by.

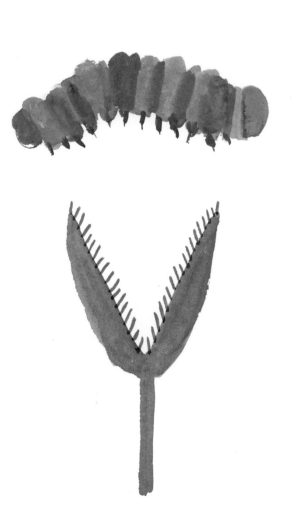

Then it ate a butterfly.

The plant grew, and so did its hunger.

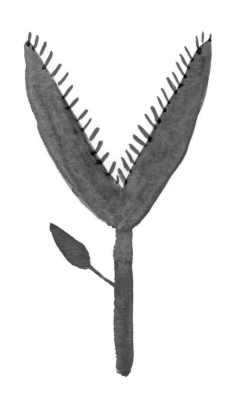

Then it ate a spider.

The plant grew, and so did its hunger.

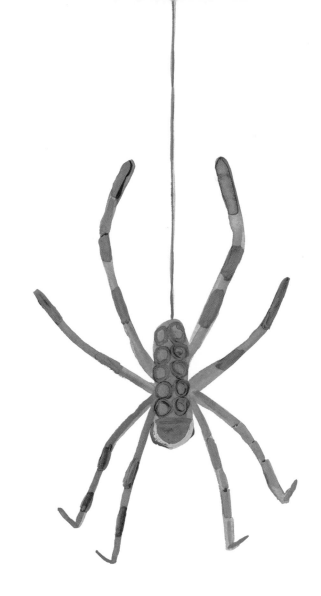

Then it ate a gecko.

The plant grew, and so did its hunger.

Then it ate a rabbit.

The plant grew, and so did its hunger.

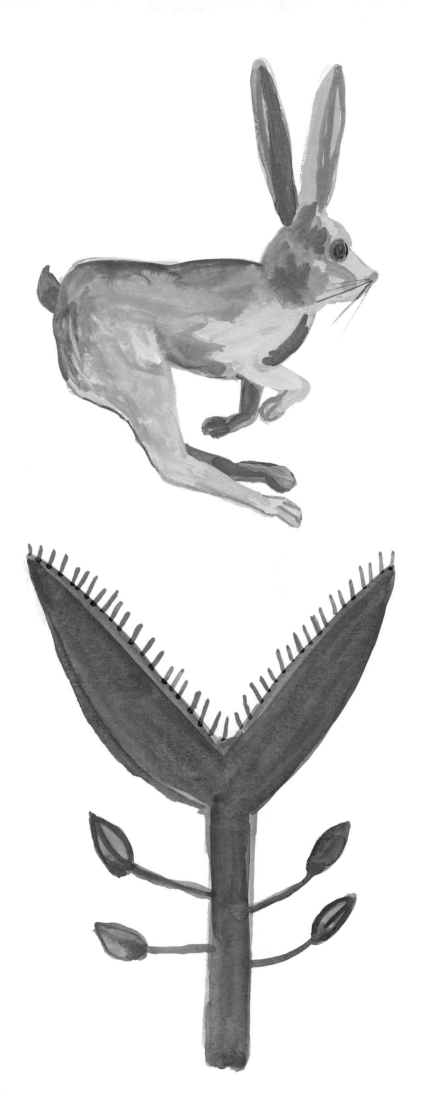

Then it ate a gymnast.

The plant grew, and so did its hunger.

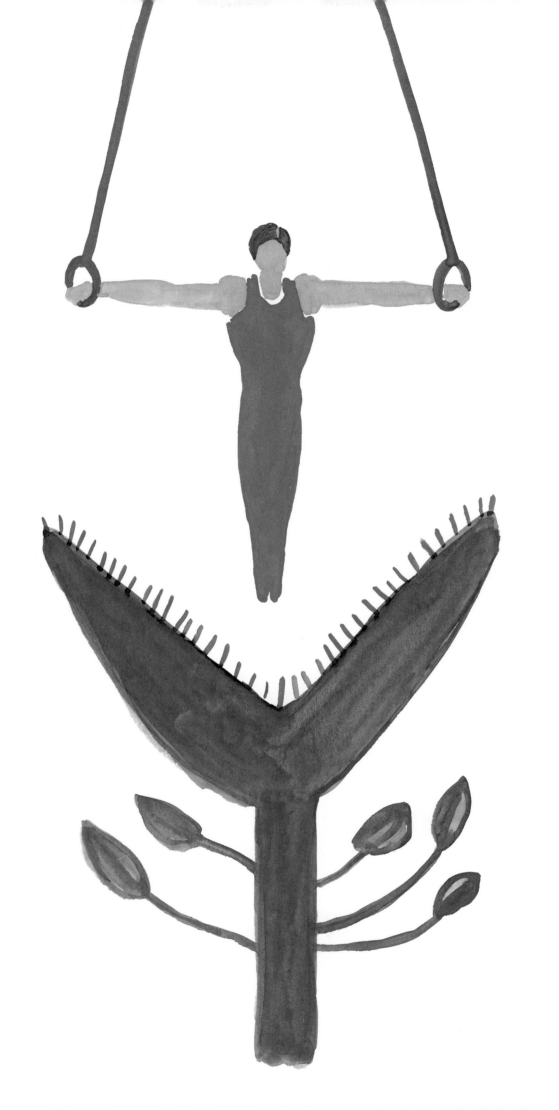

Then it ate an acrobat.

The plant grew, and so did its hunger.

Then it ate a parachutist.

The plant grew, and so did its hunger.

Then it ate an entire airplane.

The plant grew, and so did its hunger.

Then it ate a flying mammoth.

The plant grew, and so did its hunger.

Then it ate
a **bunch**
of witches.

The plant
grew, and
so did its
hunger.

Then it ate some aliens.

The plant grew, and so did its hunger.

Then it ate
a dragon.

The plant
grew, and
so did its
hunger.

Then it ate an angel choir.

The plant grew...

...but its hunger was finally satisfied, so it stopped eating and rested.

Then the carnivorous plant was eaten by a hungry herbivorous dinosaur.

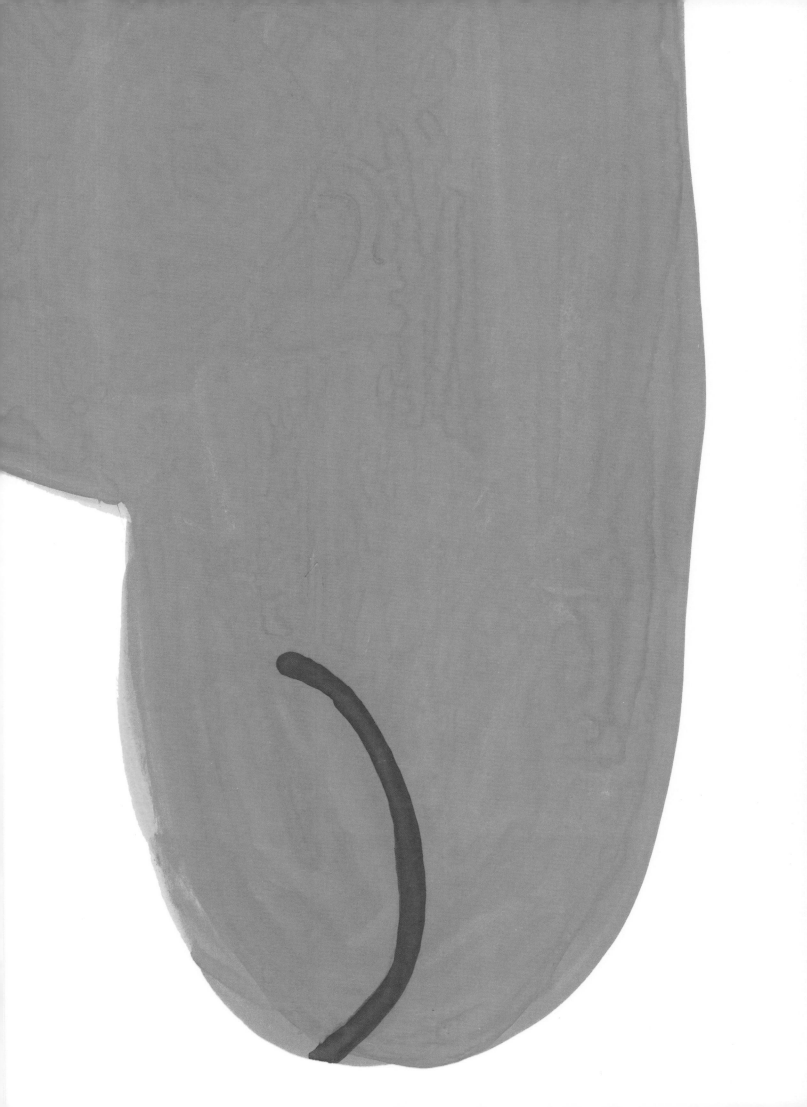

RENATO MORICONI is a Brazilian writer and visual artist. He has had more than sixty books for children published in countries around the world, including Brazil, France, Mexico, and South Korea. *The Little Barbarian* (Eerdmans), his North American debut, received multiple starred reviews and was named one of the *Boston Globe*'s best children's books of 2018.

Text and illustrations © 2021 Renato Moriconi
Published by arrangement with Debbie Bibo Agency

First published in the United States in 2021
by Eerdmans Books for Young Readers,
an imprint of Wm. B. Eerdmans Publishing Co.
Grand Rapids, Michigan

www.eerdmans.com/youngreaders

Manufactured in China

29 28 27 26 25 24 23 22 21   1 2 3 4 5 6 7 8 9

Library of Congress Cataloging-in-Publication Data

Names: Moriconi, Renato, 1980- author, illustrator.
Title: The very hungry plant / Renato Moriconi.
Description: Grand Rapids, Michigan : Eerdmans Books for Young Readers,
  2021. | Audience: Ages 3-7. | Summary: "This carnivorous plant devours
  everything in its path, but it's not the only one who's hungry"—
  Provided by publisher.
Identifiers: LCCN 2021000431 | ISBN 9780802855763 (hardcover)
Subjects: CYAC: Carnivorous plants—Fiction. | Hunger—Fiction. | Food
  habits—Fiction.
Classification: LCC PZ7.M826747 Ve 2021 | DDC [E]--dc23
LC record available at https://lccn.loc.gov/2021000431

Illustrations created with acrylic paint

THE INSPIRATION FOR THIS BOOK came when Renato's friend Paulo, owner of a vegetarian restaurant, swallowed a fly while he was yawning. With this scene in mind, Renato began to reflect on what we know and what we ignore, and how these things can affect our perception of the world around us. From that experience, Renato created this very hungry little carnivorous plant.